MIRACLE

by Jason Pinter

Illustrated by Cheryl Crouthamel

For Ava, our Miracle

For Dana, who dreamed with me

For Cheryl, who made these words come to life

For everyone who has been blessed with their own Miracle

And everyone still dreaming

Hardcover ISBN: 978-1-947993-40-2

Paperback ISBN: 978-1-947993-39-6

eISBN: 978-1-947993-38-9

Published in 2018 by Armina Press

Text copyright: Jason Pinter

Illustrations copyright: Cheryl Crouthamel

MIRACLE

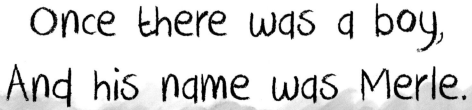

Once there was a boy,
And his name was Merle.

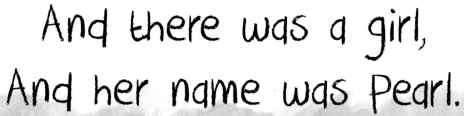

And there was a girl,
And her name was Pearl.

On one sunny day
Merle and Pearl met.

And instantly felt
That their hearts were set.

Since Merle and Pearl knew
They were birds of a feather

They made the decision to
Share life together

Now that they were a family,
They truly felt blessed
And Merle and Pearl wanted
To add to their nest.

But even though their nest was complete
They found adding to it
Was no easy feat.

For a very long time
They held off the blues,
But then it got harder
When they got some bad news.

Month after month, week after week,
Merle and Pearl's dreams were seeming quite bleak.

They tried to stay strong,
And tried not to pout, But
wherever they went They
were feeling left out.

Pursuing their dreams
Left them tired and lost.
But they would find a way,
No matter the cost.

They would search deepest oceans.

They would climb highest peaks.

They would explore farthest space.

To find what they seek.

But time trickled past,
The months came and went.

Though their dreams were still bright
Their spirit felt spent.

But suddenly one day,
As their dream's ending neared

A ray of hope came,
The clouds disappeared.

The time had been tough, the days ever long.
They prayed to each other that nothing went wrong.

But then one bright day,
Their miracle came.

The sun had come out,
replacing the rain.

The hard times they faced had felt like a test,
But with their nest expanded
They truly felt blessed.

The years had been hard,
And if they'd known then,
The long road they'd travel...

They would do it again.

Jason Pinter was born and raised in New York City and currently lives in New Jersey with his amazing wife, their miracle daughter, and their dog-slash-Ewok, Wilson. He is the founder and publisher of Polis Books, an independent publishing company, and the bestselling author of several novels for adults that his daughter won't be allowed to read for quite a while. He was named one of *Publishers Weekly*'s inagural Star Watch nominees which "recognizes young publishing professionals who have distinguished themselves as future leaders of the industry." MIRACLE is his first picture book.
isit him at www.JasonPinter.com.

Cheryl Crouthamel is a graphic artist and award winning illustrator. She spends most of her time in her home studio illustrating children's books and educational materials. When Cheryl isn't working, she's chasing her little ones and enjoying time with friends and family!
Visit her at www.CherylCrouthamel.com.

Made in United States
North Haven, CT
27 November 2021

11600066R00018